Lake
Pontchartrain

New
Orleans

Lake Borgne

Chandeleur
Sound

N

Breton
Sound

Grand
Isle

Stick

by

Steve Breen

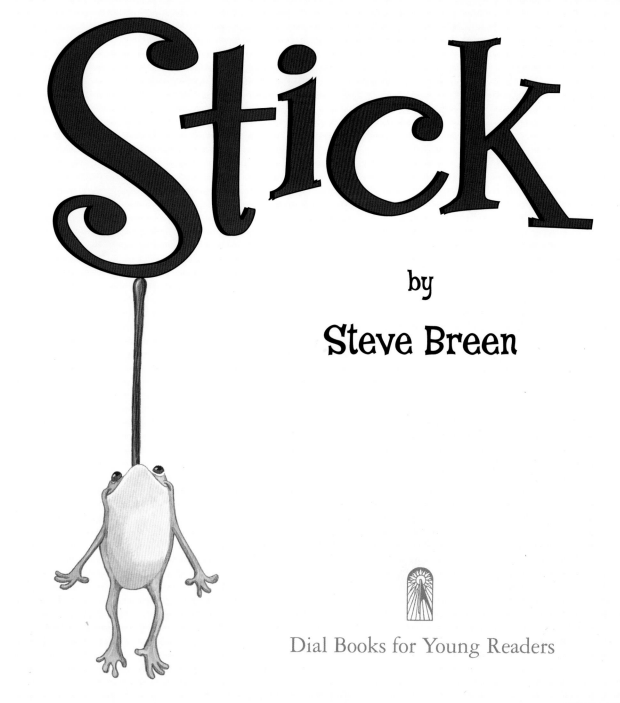

Dial Books for Young Readers

For Cathy – SB

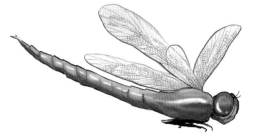

DIAL BOOKS FOR YOUNG READERS • A division of Penguin Young Readers Group •Published by The Penguin Group

Penguin Group (USA) Inc., 375 Hudson Street, New York, NY 10014, U.S.A. • Penguin Group (Canada), 90 Eglinton Avenue East, Suite 700, Toronto, Ontario, Canada M4P 2Y3 (a division of Pearson Penguin Canada Inc.) • Penguin Books Ltd, 80 Strand, London WC2R 0RL, England • Penguin Ireland, 25 St. Stephen's Green, Dublin 2, Ireland (a division of Penguin Books Ltd) • Penguin Group (Australia), 250 Camberwell Road, Camberwell, Victoria 3124, Australia (a division of Pearson Australia Group Pty Ltd) • Penguin Books India Pvt Ltd, 11 Community Centre, Panchsheel Park, New Delhi - 110 017, India • Penguin Group (NZ), Cnr Airborne and Rosedale Roads, Albany, Auckland 1310, New Zealand (a division of Pearson New Zealand Ltd) • Penguin Books (South Africa) (Pty) Ltd, 24 Sturdee Avenue, Rosebank, Johannesburg 2196, South Africa • Penguin Books Ltd, Registered Offices: 80 Strand, London WC2R 0RL, England

Designed by Lily Malcom • Text set in Fink Roman • Manufactured in China on acid-free paper

10 9 8 7 6 5 4 3 2 1

Breen, Steve.

   Stick / Steve Breen.

      p. cm.

   Summary: An independent young frog goes on a wild adventure when he accidentally gets carried away by a dragonfly.

   ISBN-13 978-0-8037-3124-0

   [1. Frogs—Fiction. 2. Dragonflies—Fiction. 3. Humorous stories.] I. Title.

   PZ7.B4822 Sti 2006

   [E]—dc22

                        2006046318

The illustrations for this book were created using watercolor and acrylic paint, colored pencil, and Photoshop.

Stick liked to do things
on his own . . .

all by himself.

One day at lunchtime . . .

And even farther away!

Through a town . . .

and into the jazzy city, he sailed.

Down
he
went . . .

and

up

again!

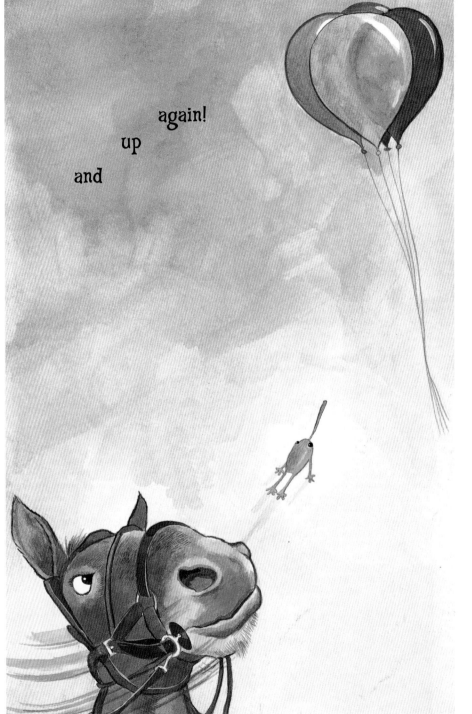

All by himself.

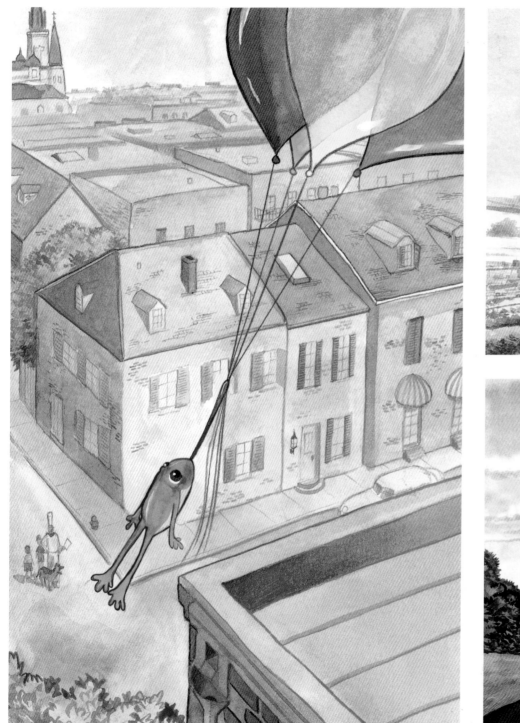

Stick flew . . .

and
fell . . .

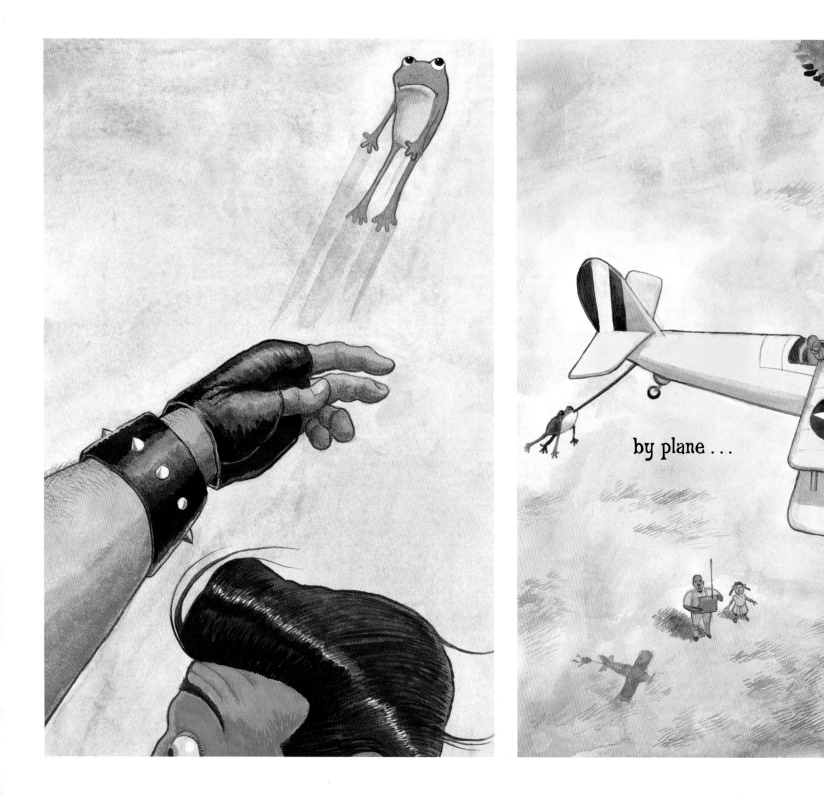

by plane . . .

and by seagull,
he traveled . . .

until Stick really was
all by himself.

It was time
to ask for help.

As the moon rose,

Stick finally found
his way . . .

And boy, was he hungry!

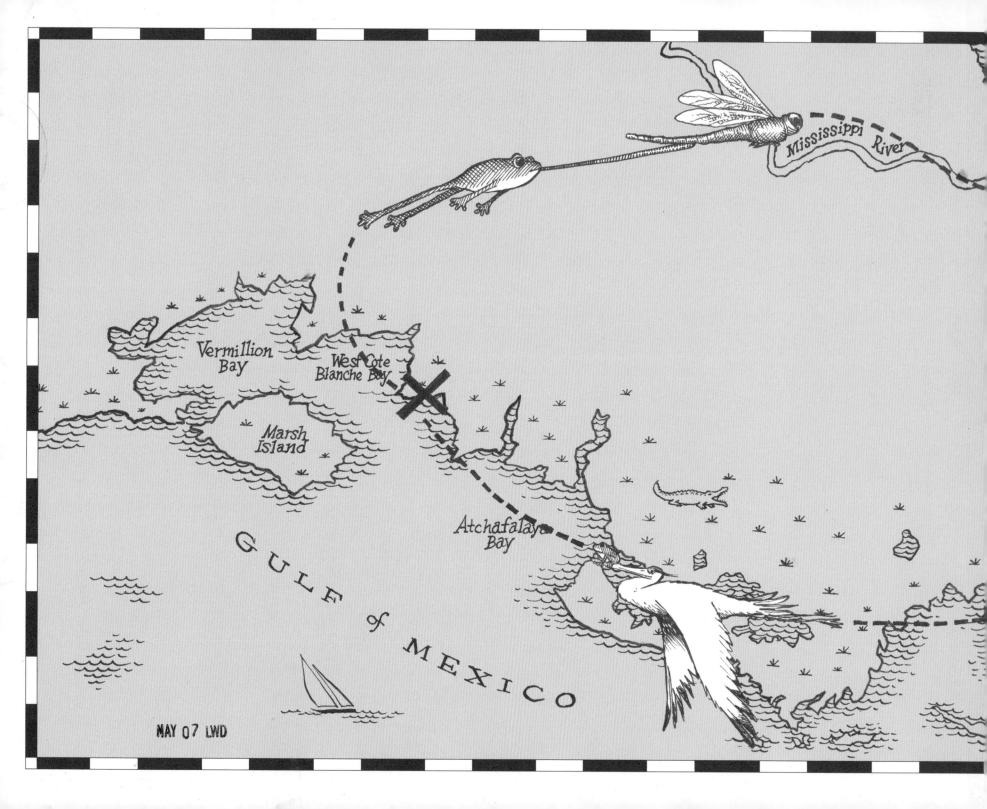

Mississippi River

Vermillion
Bay

West Cote
Blanche Bay

Marsh
Island

Atchafalaya
Bay

GULF of MEXICO

MAY 07 LWD